Lulu and Lainey

... the Lucky Day

by Lois Petren
illustrated by Tanja Russita

Other books by Lois Petren

Lulu and Lainey ... a French Yarn
Lulu and Lainey ... a Christmas Yarn

To Maggie, Bridget and Michael

ISBN-13: 978-1545473344
ISBN-10: 154547334X

It was a beautiful spring day. Lulu had just arrived at Grand-mère's apartment with her knitting basket in her hand for a visit.

"Lulu, the weather is so nice today,"
said Grand-mère. "Let's take our
knitting to the park!"

So the two of them set off with their
knitting and a picnic lunch and
walked to the Luxembourg Garden.

As they entered the
Garden they passed
the Bee House.

They heard the bees buzzing and saw them busily coming and going, doing their job of making honey.

Lulu looked forward to the honey festival in the autumn when she could taste their delicious honey.

They walked to the Great Basin- a lovely pool of water where they saw children playing with toy boats. The boats were bright and colorful in the sun.

Lulu could see the fluffy clouds and toy boats reflected in the sparkling water as the children guided them with sticks. She was amazed at how beautiful it looked.

Lulu got a boat and had a wonderful time pushing it along with her stick. She saw a mother duck gliding across the water followed by a string of ducklings.

In the middle of the pool there was a little house. The ducks swam out to it. Each of them made a little wiggle to shake the water off their feathers before they hopped through the doorway into their home.

When Lulu finished playing with her boat they continued along on their walk and passed the pony rides and the puppet theater.

They went to Lulu's favorite spot – the carousel.

She loved to ride the wooden horses and try to catch the brass ring.

Today she caught the ring for the first time.

"This is a very lucky day, Grand-mère!"

By this time they were hungry.
They found green chairs under
some trees where they could eat
and spend time knitting.

They put down their baskets and
prepared to eat their lunch.

While they ate their lunch two squirrels came running by.

Lulu and Grand-mère laughed at them as they ran up and down the trees and jumped from branch to branch while going from one tree to the next.

They ran across the ground and headed straight toward Lulu's knitting basket!

One of them landed in it and
grabbed Lulu's favorite ball of green
yarn – the one she called Lainey.

Lulu saw the little thief run off
with her favorite ball of yarn. She
got up and chased the squirrels to
get Lainey back.

But, the squirrels headed up
into the tree, taking Lainey
with them.

They went back and forth across the trees.

Eventually the yarn got stuck in the branches of the tree and the squirrel let go of Lainey.

Then they lost interest and ran off to find a new adventure.

Suddenly, a gust of wind came along, shook the branches and knocked Lainey right out of the tree. The yarn dropped down and landed at Lulu's feet.

Lulu picked it up and ran to Grand~mère. She presented Lainey and said "Grand~mère, this really is a lucky day!"

"Yes, Lulu, it certainly is," Grand~mère said with a smile.

Lulu sat back down in her chair, took out her knitting needles and started to knit. They spent a lovely afternoon knitting and chatting.

After a while Grand-mère suggested that they go to their favorite spot for hot chocolate and tea.

That's exactly what they did - to celebrate a
very lucky day!

I hope you enjoyed this book.

Be sure to visit http://www.loisapctren.com to get free coloring
pages and learn more about the world of Lulu and Lainey.

89310484R00020

Made in the USA
Middletown, DE
15 September 2018